THE BING BONG BOOK

Written by
Laura Uyeda

Illustrated by
Scott Tilley

Designed by
Tony Fejeran

🌱 A GOLDEN BOOK • NEW YORK

Copyright © 2015 Disney Enterprises, Inc., and Pixar Animation Studios. All rights reserved. Published in the United States by Golden Books, an imprint of Random House Children's Books, a division of Penguin Random House LLC, 1745 Broadway, New York, NY 10019, and in Canada by Random House of Canada, a division of Penguin Random House Ltd., Toronto, in conjunction with Disney Enterprises, Inc. Golden Books, A Golden Book, A Little Golden Book, the G colophon, and the distinctive gold spine are registered trademarks of Penguin Random House LLC.

randomhousekids.com

ISBN 978-0-7364-3321-1 (trade) — ISBN 978-0-7364-3322-8 (ebook)

Printed in the United States of America

10 9 8 7 6 5 4 3 2 1

Inside the mind of an eleven-year-old girl named Riley lived a one-of-a-kind imaginary friend.

He had the **tail** of a cat

and the **trunk** of an elephant.

He could **squeak** like a dolphin

and was made of **fluffy** cotton candy.

His name was **Bing Bong**.

One day, Bing Bong was sitting by himself in **Imagination Land,** feeling a little lonely. It had been a long time since he had played with Riley. He was worried that she had forgotten about him.

Bing Bong decided he needed to cheer himself up.

"I know! I'll have a tea party!" he said. "And I'll invite **everybody!**"

Bing Bong picked up the phone and called the **Headquarters** operator.

"Hello! I'd like to invite all the Emotions to a tea party," he said.

"All circuits are busy. Please call again," said the operator, and promptly hung up.

How strange, Bing Bong thought. *I wonder what's going on in Headquarters today. . . .*

The Emotions were in the middle of handling a crisis—Riley couldn't decide which ice cream flavor she wanted.

"Who cares?" said **Fear**. "We're going to get brain freeze no matter what!"

Bing Bong was disappointed that the Emotions couldn't join him for his tea party. But he had another idea. . . .

"I'll invite the **Forgetters!**"

He walked to **Long Term Memory,** where the Forgetters were busy sending old memories down to the dump.

"Hello, friends! Would you like to come to a tea party today?"

"**Forget it!**"

they said.

"Those guys sure are busy. That's okay. I'll go to **Dream Productions** and invite **Rainbow Unicorn**," said Bing Bong. "She's always eating donuts. . . . I bet she would love some tea cakes."

"Good afternoon, Ms. Unicorn. Would you like to come to my tea party?"

Rainbow Unicorn glanced up from her script.

"Neighhhh!" she said. Then she returned to her reading.

Bing Bong walked away, confused. "Hmmm . . . I really have to learn how to speak Unicorn."

Bing Bong left **Dream Productions** and hopped on the **Train of Thought**. He decided to ask the train engineer if he wanted to come to the tea party.

"Sorry, I've got to make some deliveries to Headquarters," the engineer said.

Bing Bong went back to **Imagination Land** by himself. He hadn't found a single friend to invite to his tea party.

Bing Bong had never felt so **lonely**.

He sat down and began to cry. Caramels, candy corn, gumballs, cinnamon swirls, saltwater taffy, lemon drops, orange gummies, peppermint puffs, raspberry bonbons, and butterscotch balls came pouring out of Bing Bong's eyes.

After a good cry, Bing Bong felt a little
better. "I'll cheer myself up with a ride in my
wagon rocket," he said.

He hopped in and began to roll down a
hill. The rocket started going

faster
and *faster*
and *faster*...

. . . until
Bing Bong
lost
control!

The rocket reached the
end of the road and fell right
into the

**Stream of
Consciousness**.

Then it floated into a tunnel.
"I've never been to this part of Imagination
Land before," said Bing Bong.

The tunnel opened up to a lush garden full of storybooks growing out of the ground. Bing Bong had discovered **Storybook Land!**

"Wow! Look at that! Riley made up these stories about me," said Bing Bong. "She remembers me after all!"

Bing Bong decided to have his tea party right there in Storybook Land. He poured himself a cup of tea and toasted the three Bing Bongs, who leaned out of their books and toasted him right back.

"Cheers!" said Jungle Bing Bong.

"Here's to you!" said Circus Bing Bong.

"Good health!" said Chef Bing Bong.

And so Bing Bong enjoyed a wonderful afternoon with three good friends: Bing Bong, Bing Bong, and Bing Bong!